# THE
# NIGHTWALKER
# CHRONICLES

# THE NIGHTWALKER CHRONICLES

*Book Three of The Immortal Chronicles Series*

# Nancy A. Lopes

Nancy A. Lopes
Visit my website at www.nancyalopesbooks.wordpress.com

Printed in the United States of America

First Printing: Jan 2019
Nancy A. Lopes Publications

ISBN 978-1-999-425-487

# Dedication

My wonderful, loving parents: I love you guys. Thank you so much for everything that you have possibly given me and all that you have done for me. I am and will be forever grateful for all of it.

To my Chroniclers, my dearest readers: You guys are the best readership in the world. These books would not be possible if not for the fact that I have you guys to read them. I am so grateful for each and every one of you. Thank you for your continued support, it means the world to me. Here's hoping that you'll like this installment as well.

# Table of Contents

The Nightwalker Chronicles

# PROLOGUE

It had been a year since the events in Vancouver and a decade before that. For the most part everything was peaceful, but if you had told me on my best friend's 26th birthday that he was the prince of a kingdom? Well, I would have thought you were crazy, but now? He's king and I couldn't be prouder. I had been at the table having my lunch when the doors opened, and Xavier entered with another body draped in his arms.

"Hey Theo, have you seen Ronan?" he asked me.

Looking at the body, I sighed. Great, another victim of these attacks; That was already the 10th one this week. Ever since someone had come in and gathered the Sanguists and used them to attack the mortals and anyone that they could again.

Shaking my head in response, I noticed to my shock and curiosity that the body in his arms had familiar long beautiful blonde hair. Getting to my feet and inching closer I soon saw to my horror who was in Xavier's arms.

"How?" I simply asked, looking up at him.

"I found her by the tower, I don't know why she was there," Xavier said.

I thought for a few minutes and then as if remembering something, my eyes widened.

"Didn't Ronan have that speech but couldn't make it, so Alexa offered to go in his place?"

"Yeah, I remember. So, you think this was a sort of revenge plot?" Xavier asked.

"What was?" a voice asked just as the doors opened again.

Turning around, we saw Ronan standing at the doors with a confused look on his face, that quickly turned to horror when his eyes fell on

Alexa. Rushing over, he carefully took her face into his palms and gazed at her, the look on his face, distraught.

"Oh Alexa…" he said, carefully looking at her face as tears grew in his eyes.

"Where did you find her?" he asked, gazing up at Xavier, his face streaked with tears.

"By the Freedom Tower. We think she may have been one of the victims of one of the latest explosions," I replied, raising a hand and placing it on his shoulder.

I pulled him into a hug allowing him to cry into my shoulder. Looking up over his head, I looked up at Xavier.

"We need to get her to the infirmary now," I said.

Nodding briefly, Xavier sped off towards the infirmary leaving just the two of us now alone together.

"Thanks, I don't know how I'm going to tell Clara and Cole their mom is gone," Ronan said.

"You're not going to do it alone. I'll be there," I replied.

"Really?"

"Of course. Do you want to tell them now?"

Ronan nodded.

"Better now than never," he said, shooting me a bleak smile.

Gently throwing an arm around his shoulders like I did when we were kids, I carefully led Ronan down the hall until he reached Clara's bedroom door. Raising a hand, I knocked on her door and waited until it opened. In the doorway, stood Clara, the look on her face, concerned.

"Dad, Uncle Theo what happened?" she asked.

Opening his mouth to speak, his eyes filled with tears. He tried many times to speak but every time Ronan tried, he just couldn't.

"Can we come in Clara? It's important," I said, noticing that Ronan was unable to fully explain what had happened.

"Of course, you can. Come in," she said, stepping back so that we could enter the room.

When we entered the room, we saw that Cole was on her bed playing with the twins. His attention was temporarily pulled away though when we entered the room.

"Hey dad, Uncle Theo did something happen?" he asked.

"Clara, can you sit down for a moment? I have to tell you and your brother something."

"Okay…Uncle Theo, you're really scaring me," Clara said.

"As I was eating lunch, Xavier came in with someone in his arms. It was your mom," I said.

"What are you saying?" Cole said, getting to his feet and walking closer.

"Your mom, she's gone," I said.

"What?"

Ronan nodded, slowly.

"Yeah, I wish it wasn't true, but it is," he said.

"But how?" Clara asked.

"We think she was one of the victims of the explosion of The Peace Tower that hit two days ago," I replied.

"What are we going to do?" Chase asked from behind Clara, his hands on her shoulders.

"We'll figure something out, don't worry."

"Theo's right, we will find out who did this and we will make them pay. Make no mistake, but for tonight? Tonight, we rest, we'll figure things out in the coming weeks," Ronan said.

"Your dad's right. Try to get some sleep," I said, offering a comforting smile.

"Okay, you too," Clara replied.

Getting to his feet, Ronan walked over to both Clara and Cole and pulled the both of them into a hug. Finally, after a few minutes, he pulled away. "Night, you guys. See you later," I replied, pulling open the door and allowed Ronan to step out ahead of me before I followed him out.

Once the two of us were out the door, I turned towards Ronan and saw that thankfully he now had a relieved smile on his face.

"You were right, that was easier than I thought. Thanks, Theo," he said.

"Of course. You had to do it, you know that Ronan. C'mon, you should get some sleep, you must be exhausted," I replied.

"You're right, I am. I guess I'll see you tomorrow, then?"

"Of course, try to get some sleep. Will you?"

"Definitely. Night Theo."

"Night Ronan."

We gave each other one final wave and headed back to our separate rooms. Once I reached mine, my hand grasped the doorknob and opened it, stepping into the room. Shirking off my clothes and boots, I pulled back the covers and got into bed, falling asleep soon after.

1

# CHAPTER ONE

T heo, Xavier and several others were in the city headed towards the middle of the city to help clear some things up a few days later. A worker at the city's bloodwork services had asked Ronan if he could send a few people to help clear some stuff out which he quickly agreed to do so. A few minutes later, the group was just outside the Bloodwork Services building and entered it. They found to their amazement, no one was there.

"What the hell, didn't you say that Ronan wanted us to come here?" Xavier asked Theo, looking over at him.

"Yeah, that's what he told me. What do you say, do you want to look around?"

"May as well, see what we find and all."

"Alright, let's get going then."

They had made sure to be careful when moving throughout the building since they didn't want to alert anything that shouldn't be alerted of their presence in the first place. Moving throughout the hallways, that soon changed when they heard extremely weak calls for help coming from behind one of the doors. Curious now, they were alarmed at what they saw when they opened the door and entered. In the room were cells large enough to fit a few people in them, but now had one-two corpses laying in them.

"What the... did Ronan know that this was here?" Xavier asked Theo.

He shrugged.

"I don't think so," he said.

Taking another look around, he went further into the cell and found hooked along the walls, long rubber tubes that had long sharp needles at the end of them. Confused, he stepped back and stuck his head back out again.

"Hey Xavier, can you come here for a minute?" Theo asked.

Xavier walked towards where Theo was and poked his head into the cell that he'd been standing in. He quickly spotted the odd tubes and upon seeing them, made a quick decision.

"C'mon we need to get back. Ronan needs to know about this," he said.

"Are you sure?"

"Yeah."

He stepped back so that Theo could step through the cell door and so they could head back to the castle. A few minutes later, they were out the doors of the Bloodwork Services building and headed towards the castle.

Ronan had been pouring over a large map that was spread over his desk and gazed intently at it, deciding what he was going to do. His mind was troubled, just as it was when everything had started. Because of the chaos that had erupted, any remaining mortals had moved towards either the small buildings or in certain cases, the islands in order to avoid becoming someone's next meal.

The doors of his office slammed open and Theo ran in, looking alarmed. Stopping in front of his best friend, he placed a hand on his shoulder. Ronan turned around, his eyebrows raised, he wondered what had his friend so alarmed.

"Theo, what happened?" he asked.

"I need to speak to you now, Ronan," Theo replied.

"Of course, Follow me," Ronan replied.

Getting to his feet, he moved around Theo and headed out the door with Theo closely following behind him.

"You wouldn't believe what we found, Ronan," Theo replied, taking a deep breath once they entered his office.

"What did you find Theo?" Ronan asked.

"Did you know about the Blood Services building?" Theo asked.

"What about it?" he asked, with a confused frown.

"It's been completely ransacked. Did you know that it was used as a place to harvest mortal blood?" Theo asked.

"Are you sure?" Ronan asked.

"You didn't know?" Theo asked.

"No, of course not," Ronan replied.

"What are we going to do?"

"For now? Best to lay low. We'll figure out a better course of action later."

"Alright."

Getting to their feet, the two of them walked to the doorway of Ronan's office.

"Thanks for letting me know, Theo," Ronan said.

"You'd do the same for me think nothing of it."

Just as Theo was about to leave Ronan grabbed his shoulder and pulled him back.

"Hey, do you want to stay and have dinner with us?"

"Unfortunately, I can't. I have to get going."

"Really?"

"I have some things I need to take care of," he replied.

He was just turning to leave when Ronan called him back again.

"Hey Theo, could you speak to Mackenzie and let them know that both of you will be going into the city with me."

"I'll tell them in the morning."

"Thanks, Theo."

"No problem. See you tomorrow."

Ronan bid his friend goodbye and watched as Theo left. He then went back to looking at the map on his desk, at which he remained until he headed to bed that night.

The next morning, Theo awoke and headed down to the dining room where he found Mackenzie sitting at the table eating breakfast. Approaching them, Theo smiled at Mackenzie as their eyes met his. He took a seat across from them and watched as they ate breakfast and eventually put their plate aside.

Over the course of that year, Mackenzie had kept in touch with Matteo, the Alpha from Vancouver and they made sure to call each other every weekend. Their relationship was still going strong, and both of them wanted to see one another as soon as possible.

"Morning, Theo."

"Good Morning. Ronan wanted me to ask you something," he replied.

"What's wrong?" Mackenzie asked, raising an eyebrow.

"There was another attack yesterday and Ronan wanted me to ask you something," he replied.

"What's wrong?" Mackenzie asked, raising an eyebrow.
"There was another attack yesterday and Ronan wanted to head into the city and see if there were any survivors."

"Just let me get ready and I'll meet you, okay?" Mackenzie replied, with a nod.

"Alright."

Mackenzie ran up to their room and grabbed a green shirt, black jeans and a matching green belt. Pulling on their shirt and jeans, they finally put on their belt, getting to their feet they pulled on their favourite black leather boots. Once they were fully dressed, they left their room and headed back down to the dining room where they found Ronan and Theo waiting.

"Got everything you need, kid?" he asked, pulling them into a brief hug. He glanced briefly at the purple and green backpack that was seated uncomfortably on Mackenzie's shoulders.

"Yeah, are you?"

"Yep."

"Theo, let's go."

Leaving the dining room, they passed Xavier who happened to be playing with Clara's twins and left the castle and headed into the city. In the past few decades, Toronto had slowly begun rebuilding to its former glory and many parts of the city looked as if the outbreak from all those centuries ago had never even happened.

The exterior of the hospital consisted of various buildings that were decrepit and run down, the buildings closest to the street were the ones that took the worst hit while the buildings near the far back almost didn't suffer any damage whatsoever. The three of them had walked in and began to run through the halls towards where the cries were coming from, where the emergency room was.

Nancy A. Lopes

# CHAPTER TWO

O nce  they were in, they searched each room until they reached a small room where they found a young girl with shoulder-

length dirty blonde hair and murky blue eyes, gazing up at them. The

moment though that her eyes fell on Mackenzie, her expression changed

to one of shock.

"Mackenzie is that really you?" she asked, still in shock.

Equally, in shock, Mackenzie began to slowly walk closer towards her when suddenly Theo placed a gentle hand on their chest.

"Kimberly?"

"I thought you'd died," she replied, still in shock.

"How do you know Mackenzie?" Theo asked her, easing his grip slightly. "Kimberly was a part of the village that I had stayed in when I was a kid. We practically grow up together," Mackenzie replied, turning to Theo.

"What are you doing here?" they asked, turning toward Kimberly.

"I got trapped here."

"Really?"

Kimberly nodded.

"Oh, how rude of me. Kimberly, these are my friends, Theo and Ronan," they replied.

Glancing at both men, Kimberly smiled, slightly.

"Hello," she said.

"Are you hurt Kimberly, is that why you were here when we got here?" Mackenzie asked.

"I'm not hurt, no."

"What are you doing here?" Theo asked.

"Miles wanted us to see if there are more survivors from the latest attacks."

"You seem to have been trapped here would you like for us to help us to help you get out of here?" he asked Kimberly.

Surprised, she nodded.

With Mackenzie's help, they put Kimberly back into the wheelchair that was laying on its side a few steps away. The three of them walked out of the room with Mackenzie pushing her chair out of the hospital. Once they reached the exterior of the hospital, Kimberly turned around to face the three of them.

"I'll talk to Miles and see what he says," she said to them.

"Thanks. I'm gonna speak to our group and see how we can help. Do you want to meet up in three days' time?" he said.

"Sure," Kimberly replied.

1

"Alright, see you when I see you," Mackenzie replied, smiling.

Stepping closer to Kimberly and pulled her into a tight hug, they finally after a few brief moments separated and Mackenzie walked back over to where Theo and Ronan were. Reaching them both, they turned around and raised a hand, waving goodbye. Kimberly waved back and then wheeled off towards where her group's camp was.

Once she was out of sight, the three of them turned and made their way back towards the castle. Making their way through the city, they soon reached the castle's gates with Xavier standing at them. Seeing them, his lips stretched into a bright smile.

"Hey guys, did you have a successful mission?" he said.

Ronan nodded.

"I need to gather everyone. We need to talk about some stuff," he said.

"I'll go now. Where do you want us?" Xavier replied, raising an eyebrow, questioningly.

"Get everyone in the main hall and I'll meet you there."

Xavier nodded briefly and turned on his heel, heading back into the castle. When he was gone, Ronan turned to Mackenzie and Theo.

"Do you both want to be there when I tell everyone what happened?" he asked them.

"Of course," they both replied in unison.

15 minutes later, everyone was gathered in a large group in the castle's main hall, Mackenzie and Theo had chosen to hang off to the side. The main hall was a large, spacious modern-styled room that was brightly lit by LED lights and had a very well-built platform where Ronan was currently standing on. He waited until the noise in the room had quieted down and began once it did.

"I found out some things when we went into the city today," he said, "as it turns out there are some mortals that have managed to keep themselves alive," he continued, "they were looking for answers as to why everything had gotten so bad exactly. So, in three days, I'll be meeting with the girl that we met today, and she'll be bringing someone with her as well."

1

Near the back of the group, a slightly tall young man who had short strawberry blonde hair and blueish-green eyes raised a hand.

"Um, meaning no offense your excellency, but who's the girl? How do we know that we can trust her?" he asked.

Mackenzie stepped forward and moved to Ronan's side so that they could explain what had happened properly.

"I've known Kimberly my whole childhood. She and I lived together when I was younger and living at the village that took me in after my mother was killed," they said.

"So, she can be trusted?"

"Absolutely."
The man still looked doubtful, stepping back into the crowd.

"Any other questions?" Ronan asked, looking around at everyone.

"Very well. Mackenzie, Theo and I will be heading back into the city and we'll be meeting with Kimberly and her friend in a few days and we'll just see how big the problem is," he said when no one replied.

Once he'd finished speaking, Ronan dismissed the group and told them to get some sleep, he was sure they were going to need it for what was coming in the next few days.

Nancy A. Lopes

# CHAPTER THREE

Three days later, Mackenzie, Ronan, and Theo arrived back at just outside the hospital grounds. This time around, when they arrived, they saw that Kimberly was accompanied by another familiar face to Mackenzie.

Miles Andrews stood at five-foot-eleven and had short light brown hair and warm blue eyes. He had a lean build and the look that he had currently on his face was a mixture of disbelief and awe. Slowly, he approached Mackenzie and brought them into a tight hug and began to sob as he did so. He knew he shouldn't have let them get separated in the first place as he had.

"I'm so sorry for leaving you, Mackenzie. I should never have done so," Miles said, once he'd wiped their tears away.

1

"It's alright, I mean I was the one who wandered off and got lost. I forgive you," Mackenzie replied.

"I hate to cut in guys, but I wanted to ask your friend here something," Ronan said, smiling warmly at the both of them.

Blushing profusely, Mackenzie traded glances between Miles and Ronan.

"Guys, this is Miles, he's the one who looked after me when my mom died when I was a kid."

"Nice to meet you. I'm Ronan and this is Theo," Ronan replied.

"Likewise."

"I wanted to ask you something, Miles," Ronan said, his eyebrows furrowed slightly.

"I was wondering if you'd noticed all the attacks that have been going on?"

"Notice them? We nearly lost two of our people in the last set of explosions," Miles replied.

"Really?" Mackenzie asked.

"Yeah, it was horrible. Why do you ask?" he asked.

"I was wondering if maybe you'd accept staying at the castle for a while."

The look on Miles' face grew suddenly cold as if a switch had gone on his features.

"The castle, so you're a Fanger, is that it, are you all Fangers?" Miles asked.

"No just Mackenzie and I are. Theo's a Lycan but we won't hurt you," Ronan replied.

"Oh really?"

"Yes! Look Miles, Ronan's father was King Garrett, not President Adams. You remember him, don't you?" Mackenzie protested.

The anger disappeared from his face as he nodded.

"I do. He was a good man. I'm so sorry, Ronan. Please forgive me?" Miles said.

"Of course. And the offer still stands if you'd like?'

Miles nodded.

"When should we be there?" he asked.

"How about in two days, does that sound good?" Ronan asked.

"For sure. We'll be there."

"See you guys later. Nice to have met you both."

Going their opposite ways, Miles and Kimberly headed to their camp while Mackenzie, Ronan, and Theo headed back to the castle. When they got back, Ronan knew that he needed to speak with Xavier as soon as possible.

When they reached the castle, Ronan spotted Xavier and pulled him aside, so he could speak to him.

"How can I help you, Ronan?" Xavier asked, following him into his office. He took a seat right across and watched as Ronan closed the door and took a seat.

"Do you remember how we met again with that girl, Kimberly?"

Xavier nodded.

"Well, this time she brought the leader of her camp with her. There's one more thing."

"Oh?"

"I invited them to stay here at the castle," Ronan replied.

Taking a deep breath, Xavier waited a few moments before speaking. He wanted to be careful when choosing his words and took great caution in what he said next to his godson.

"Do you think that's such a smart idea, Ronan?" he asked, his eyebrows were knit in confusion.

"We can use all the help we can get, Uncle Xavier. And they seem like they really need our help as well."

"Really, how so?" Xavier asked.

"They're mortals, Uncle Xavier."

"What?" he asked, quietly.

"I have to ask you, Ronan, have you gone completely insane?" Xavier nearly shouted, throwing his hands in the air in alarm. He got up, sharply and stood behind his chair, his hands now gripping it tightly.

"No, I have not. These mortals are Mackenzie's kin," he replied, getting to his feet calmly. Ronan leveled Xavier with an intense look.

"I'm sorry. I think I heard you wrong," Xavier said, looking at him in disbelief.

"You didn't. This guy, Miles raised Mackenzie," Ronan said.

Taking a deep breath, it was a while before Xavier spoke.

"I have just one more question."

"Of course."

"Can we trust them?" Xavier asked, finally after a while.

"Absolutely. With what I saw between him and Mackenzie I wouldn't doubt that we can most definitely trust them," Ronan didn't hesitate to reply.

"Alright, do you want me to tell the others?"

Ronan nodded.

"Okay," Xavier replied.

"Thank you. Goodnight, Uncle Xavier."

Shooting him a brief smile, Xavier turned on his heel and started to leave the room, when he paused for a moment.

"Night, Ronan."

2

Once the door was closed and Xavier had left, Ronan took a moment to just get along or at the very least be civil.

# CHAPTER FOUR

A few days later Miles' group arrived. He smiled once he saw Ronan walking closer to them.

"Thank you again for letting us stay here," he said.

"It's my pleasure and thanks for helping us out. I swear none of you will be harmed while you are here, you have my word," Ronan replied.

Reaching inside, they stopped when they reached the main hall. All of those in Miles' group seemed to be gazing at the others rather nervously.

"I'd like to thank you for joining us here at our home and agreeing to help us solve this problem that has put the city into such danger. You'll be getting your rooms while you're here, as well as anything you need," Ronan said.

Miles smiled, stepping closer.

2

"It's our pleasure. May I say a few words?" he asked.

"Of course."

Stepping down, Ronan allowed Miles to take his place, curious as to what he could possibly have to say.

"My dear friends, I'd like to thank Ronan for having us here as my guests. It's very much appreciated. There's one last thing, Mackenzie would you please come up here?" he said.

To Mackenzie's surprise, they got to feet and walked to where Miles stood. As they did so, Mackenzie couldn't help but notice the fact that everyone was whispering amongst each other. Finally, they reached where Miles was standing and turned towards the others.

"Hey everyone, it's so nice to see you after all this time. I really missed all of you, it's good to be back here among all of you," they said.

After Mackenzie spoke, they walked back to their previous spot and Ronan in turn, took up where Mackenzie had been standing.

"I've arranged for a few rooms to be available for you while you're here. Now, if you'll follow me, I'd like to show you to your rooms," he said.

Heading down the halls, they continued to walk until they stopped just outside the bedrooms where they would be residing in.

"These rooms, just as I said before, are for your use. You guys can use these rooms and make them your own while you're here, I hope you enjoy them. You guys should get settled since dinner will be ready soon," he said.

Smiling, he let them get themselves settled until he called them down for dinner after which they headed to bed ready for a long day.

The following morning, they got up and ready. Ronan and Miles suggested that they head into the city to see if they could see if there were any clues as to why the city's blood supply was disappearing so quickly.

A few minutes later, they were within the city limits and split up into groups of two or three. While there, Ronan, Theo, and Mackenzie headed into an abandoned school and began searching it. As they were looking for survivors, they eventually split up and Mackenzie headed into one of the classrooms. They had been looking around when suddenly they heard a rustling sound coming from behind them.

2

"Theo, Ronan is that you?"

When they didn't hear a word and the rustling continued until Mackenzie saw what had caused the noise. Standing some mere inches from their face, saliva dripping from its snout, was a massive half shifted Lycan. It stood at six-foot-seven, had unkempt dirty blonde hair and dead-looking blue eyes. Like most of its kind, he had a massive build that was now crouched as he watched them, as a low growl built up in his chest. The clothes he was wearing were torn and unkempt in some places since he'd probably lived on the streets.

Thinking quickly, Mackenzie began to look for a possible makeshift weapon. Finding one, they quickly sped past the Lycan and picked up the stones that they spotted there and spun on their heel, throwing a few of them passed the Lycan which managed to infuriate it even more. Letting out a loud, frightening roar, the Lycan moved towards Mackenzie and took a swipe which they narrowly missed. Seeing the situation that they now put themselves in, Mackenzie quickly hid behind an old teacher's desk that was up front and called out for help.

"Theo, Ronan, help me!" Mackenzie yelled.

The Lycan continued to attack them when suddenly it got thrown off Mackenzie by a large shadow. Curious as to what it could have been, they raised their head slightly and saw to their shock both Theo and the Lycan locked in a ferocious battle.

"Mackenzie! Don't move I'm gonna come to you!" a voice came from over their shoulder.

Slowly turning their head, they saw Ronan running over to them, the look on his face, clearly frightened. Once he reached Mackenzie he knelt down and carefully scooped them up into his arms. When Mackenzie was in Ronan's arms, he quickly got to his feet and sped off towards the castle. Just as they reached it, Mackenzie fainted from their injuries. Ronan took a moment and carefully put them down for a few minutes. He then removed his shirt and ripped it in two and used it to staunch the bleeding that had already begun forming. Picking them up, he held the shirt to Mackenzie's leg and ran towards the castle.

When he finally reached the castle, he ran in and was elated when he came across his daughter, Clara.

"Oh, thank God Clara, I'm so glad that I found you," Ronan said in relief.

"Dad, what happened to Mackenzie?" Clara asked, looking at them in alarm, ready to help any way that she could.

1

"Mackenzie got attacked while we were in the city, we just got there we found them with their leg mangled."

"Alright, follow me. We have to get Mackenzie to the infirmary, so we can bandage it."

Turning, Clara led them down the hall and towards the infirmary. Entering it, he carefully placed Mackenzie on one of the beds while Clara went and grabbed a few things. Heading back to their bed, Clara now had bandages and a small metal bowl in her hands. Reaching them, she carefully put the bowl down and reached into it and pulled out an old dirty gray rag. Wringing it, Clara began to gently clean Mackenzie's leg up.

Once their leg was cleaned up, Clara began to slowly bandage up Mackenzie's leg and made sure she took extreme care as she did. She didn't want to injure the leg any more than she needed to or risk the possibility of it catching an infection.

Just then the door opened and in walked Miles and Theo who upon spotting where Theo was standing, rushed over. Miles took a seat on Mackenzie's bed and took their hand, the look on Miles' face understandably distraught.

"How could I let this happen?" he asked.

"It's not your fault, Miles. If anything, it's our fault for leaving them," Ronan replied.

"You're right, this is all your fault. How could you have been so irresponsible!" Miles shot back, whipping around to furiously face him.

"I know and we're sorry," Theo said, earnestly.

"Apology accepted. Would it be alright if I stayed with Mackenzie, just for the night?"

"Of course. You don't need to ask. Do you want any help with bringing one of the beds closer?" Ronan asked.

"No thanks, I'll be alright. You guys should get some rest," Miles said, with a small smile.

"Okay, have a good night Miles," Ronan said, walking towards the door. His hand was on the doorknob when Miles spoke again.

"Night, guys."

Opening the door, Theo and Ronan left the room, heading towards their individual rooms so that they could get some much-needed rest.

# CHAPTER FIVE

oughly about three months of watching Mackenzie slowly
getting better, Theo and Ronan walked into the infirmary with
two hot cups of coffee in their hands. They nearly dropped them though
when they saw that Mackenzie had awoken. Rushing over, they gently
placed the cups down on the bedside table and frantically began to look
them over to see if they were okay.

Guys, guys! I'm fine!" Mackenzie said, trying to get the both of them to
calm down and back away, with a light laugh and a warm smile on their
face.

"We're so glad that you're okay Mac," Theo said.

"How do you feel?" Ronan said.

"Kind of sore. What happened?" they asked, wincing slightly.

"You don't remember?" Theo asked.

"Not really. The only thing that I remember is the Lycan that was standing over me."

"Yeah, well it tore into your leg."

"Really?"

"I had to grab you and bring you back here, otherwise you wouldn't have made it," Ronan replied.

Theo nodded.

"Hey Mac, are you hungry?" Ronan asked.

"Yeah a bit," Mackenzie replied.

"Alright, tell you what. I'm gonna grab some food and see if I can find Miles," Theo said.

"Okay, thanks."

Getting to his feet, he pulled both Mackenzie and Ronan into a quick hug and left.

When Theo had left, Ronan turned back towards Mackenzie.

"Is there anything else I can get you?" Ronan asked.

"Can we watch a movie?" Mackenzie asked, smiling slightly.

"Of course, we can. Just let me get everything ready."

"Okay."

Ronan walked over to where an old-looking television was placed against the far-left wall which was just opposite to them. It came with a player as well as the film canisters placed upon it. Picking up the first film, he put it into the player and started it. Once the film was in, Ronan took a seat on one of the other beds and soon they were enjoying the film. They laughed, cried, but overall, they thoroughly enjoyed the two films.

Two hours later, they were playing cards when Cole walked in, a concerned on his face and his hands in his pockets.

"Hey, son, what brings you here?" Ronan asked.

"I wanted to check in and see how Mackenzie was doing. Dad, if you wanted to grab something to eat, you can. I'll look after them while you're gone," he said.

"Are you sure?" Ronan asked.

"Yeah, it's fine. Go right ahead."

"Thanks, son," he said, with a grateful smile.

He got to his feet, hurrying out the door and towards the kitchen. When his father left, Cole turned towards Mackenzie with a smile on his face.

"So, you want to play a round of cards?" he asked.

"Sure, I'd love to."

Over the course of the past hour, the two of them played a rousing game of cards.

About a few hours later, Theo and Miles walked into the room and saw Mackenzie sitting up, playing cards with Cole.

"Where's Ronan?" Theo asked.

Cole turned towards Theo his spot on the hospital bed.

"Hey Uncle Theo, I told him to get something to eat. He looked like he could use it," he replied with a smile.

"Alright, I'll just stay here then. Oh, Mackenzie, I brought you some food to eat," Theo replied.

"He passed them a plastic bag that was filled with several tupperwares of food. Opening it, he removed each container and headed them to Mackenzie.

"I got all your favourites, Mackenzie. I hope you like them," Theo smiled uncertainly.

"Thank you for all of this, it looks so good," Mackenzie said, gratefully.

Mackenzie began to eat from each of the tupperwares, which contained a variety of foods from salad to a small bowl that had a delicious pasta with bits of chicken in it that was drizzled in mayonnaise, while another of the bowls had some French fries and onion rings in it. They continued to go back and forth between containers until they finished them.

"Thank you for all this. It was delicious, I loved everything. I really appreciated it," they said.

"You're welcome, Mac. It's my pleasure."

When Mackenzie had finished, they put all the tupperwares aside just as Miles pulled them into a tight hug.

"I'm so glad to see that you're better."

Mackenzie nodded.

"Yeah, I think so. I really appreciate all this, guys. I should be ready by tomorrow," they said.

"That's good."

Theo had gotten to his feet over the course of Mackenzie and Miles' conversation and walked over to one of the windows in the infirmary and looked out at the now night sky.

"Hey guys, it's getting late we should get going. Mac, we'll come back in the morning to pick you up, okay?" he said.

"Alright, night guys. See you tomorrow," Mackenzie said, smiling.

Cole and Miles pulled Mackenzie into a hug and wished them goodnight and left. Finally, Theo pulled Mackenzie into a hug.

"Get some sleep. I'll be back in the morning."

"Okay, night Theo," Mackenzie replied, with a small smile, snuggling into their sheets, just a bit more.

"Night Mac," Theo said, placing a gentle kiss on their forehead and stepped back walking towards the door, giving Mackenzie one final wave. He then opened the door and left, closing it quietly behind it. When he got back to his room, he got into bed and soon fell asleep afterward.

Nancy A. Lopes

# CHAPTER SIX

The following morning back at the infirmary, Mackenzie awoke and got ready. They decided to wear blue jeans today and their usual favourite green top, black leather jacket, and black combat boots. They didn't have to wait long for Theo to arrive as he soon came into the infirmary, his hands holding two cups; one with tea and the other with coffee.

"Good Morning Mac. Want to get breakfast? I think Miles asked one of the ladies to make a delicious breakfast for you," Theo said, with a smile. He passed the cup of tea to Mackenzie while he, in turn, held onto the coffee.

"Really? Wow, I need to thank him," Mackenzie replied, with a smile, taking the tea, gratefully.

"Let's go, then."

A few minutes later, both of them were downstairs in the dining room. The beautiful oak table that was situated in it had plates of pancakes and other things, bowls of various things as well as a few pitchers of several beverages such as milk and juice.

To Mackenzie's absolute elation, they saw that Miles had stayed behind to wait for them. Taking a seat, they began to take a little of everything; all the food that had been laid out had been laced with blood.

"All of this is so delicious!" Mackenzie said, looking at Miles, gratefully.

"Thank you," said a woman who was standing near Miles, lips curled into a warm smile.

She was African-American, had lovely light brown eyes and short wild mahogany brown hair and was thin and had kind features.

"You made all this?" Mackenzie asked, surprised.

"I did."

"Thank you. As I said, it's very good."

Miles placed a hand on the woman's shoulder, smiling warmly.

"This is Sarah, she made all the food that's here," he said.

"It's nice to meet you. I hope you're comfortable here," Ronan said.

"I am. Thank you, your excellency," she said.

"Good. Hey Miles, I was thinking about looking through the city again to see if we can find anyone else," Ronan said.

"That sounds like a wonderful idea. Did you just want us to go or will we be going with anyone else?" Miles replied.

"If it's alright with you, I'd like for Theo and Mackenzie to go with us."

"Are you okay with that, Mackenzie?"

"Me? I'm alright. I'd like to go into the city too," Mackenzie replied.

They had gone to the city's south side and came across one of the hospitals there. Opening the doors, they took extreme care in entering the building. Suddenly, they heard voices coming from a separate part of the foyer they were in. Feeling curious, the four of them followed the voices until they found the source of it. Standing in front of them, wearing black hooded robes that had red trim, was a small group of young men who were watching them, wearily. Mackenzie was shocked when they saw their brother, Chase among them, now looking years older.

Chase, who was now 18 years old, and now stood at six feet tall. He had short windswept raven black hair and usually vibrant blue eyes that seemed to have dulled over some time.

4

"Chase is that really you?" they asked.

The stoic look that Chase had on his face dropped for a moment and was replaced with one of confusion.

"Do I know you?" he asked.

"I'm your sibling, I'm Mackenzie."

"I don't have a sibling."

"Yes, you do!"

"But he said I didn't have any family."

"Who?"

"Dylan, the man who took me in."

Mackenzie knew that they had to do something to help Chase out and fast since what mattered now was helping their brother remember. They didn't waste any time in speeding over to him and carefully approached him.

"I think Dylan lied to you."

"What, that can't be!" Chase exclaimed.

Mackenzie gently took his shoulder.

"It may be. Look at me, really look at me. Don't we look alike?" they asked.

Chase slowly looked at them, this time really looking at them. Finally, they knew that they had gotten through to him when recognition swam into his eyes.

"Mackenzie how?" he croaked out.

"It's so good to see you, baby brother," Mackenzie replied, carefully pulling Chase into a hug.

"Same here. I can't believe Dylan lied to me."

"So, you've been staying with him?"

Chase nodded.

"Well, now that you found me you don't have to stay with him."

"But I do, Mackenzie."

"Why do you feel indebted to him?"

"You know why," Chase replied.

Mackenzie thought for a moment, trying to figure out what they could do to possibly help Chase.

4

"Hey, Mac, why don't I stop by once a month every month? That way no one will suspect me stopping by and visiting," Chase asked, jostling them out of their thoughts.

"Are you sure? I wouldn't want you getting hurt."

"Don't worry about me, Mackenzie. I can take care of myself."

"You shouldn't have to, Chase."

Suddenly though, there was an odd rustling noise that was close to where they all were. The others ran off so unfortunately Chase and Mackenzie had to cut their conversation short.

C'mon Mackenzie, we have to go now!" yelled Theo, from behind them.

"I've got to go, Chase, we'll see each other soon?" Mackenzie asked. "Soon. I love you, Mac," Chase replied with a small smile, pulling them into a hug. Finally, they pulled apart and went their separate ways.

Mackenzie looked back once again over their shoulder and saw that a Lycan had emerged from the bushes.

Half an hour later, they decided to see how things were at the castle and found to their absolute horror that it had been burned to the ground. Reaching where the remains now were, Ronan began to look around frantically; he needed to make sure everyone was alive and well. He felt like he was going to sob in relief when he saw that Clara was alive. Running over, he pulled her into a tight hug.

"Where is everyone?" he asked his daughter.

"Those of us that could get out is over there," Clara said, leading her father down a path that was near the west wall of where the castle once stood.

Those that had managed to survive stood in a small group off to the side as they approached them. Aaron who had been standing with the others walked up to him and placed a hand on Ronan's shoulder, a grim expression on his face.

"What happened Aaron?" he asked.

"We don't know Ronan, just that the castle is gone. Everything is gone," Aaron said.

"Do you know where Xavier is? I need to speak to him."

"He went to go check on everyone and see if they were alright," he said.

"Okay, I'm going to go find him. I'll be back," he said.

Ronan got to his feet and began to move around their group, looking for Xavier; He found him a short while later speaking to Miles.

"Hey guys, can I speak to the both of you?" Ronan asked.

"Of course," Xavier replied.

"Sure," Miles replied.

"Do you guys have any clue what happened?" Ronan asked.

"The castle just burst into flames. If it wasn't for Xavier and Aaron, I think we might have died to be honest," Miles replied.

"So, you didn't see who caused the fire?"

"No, we didn't see anyone. We only saw that a fire had spread throughout the castle when we arrived here," Xavier replied.

"If you'd like you guys can stay with us, it's the least that we could do," Miles said.

"Would you really let us stay with you?" Ronan asked.

"Of course. Anything you need, it'll be there. We promise."

"We'd love to. Just let me tell everyone, okay?"

"I'll do it, Ronan. Don't worry, I'll be right back," Xavier said, speeding off in search of the others.

"It should be fine with them, we don't really have any other options, to be honest."

"What should be fine with them?" a voice said from behind Ronan.

Mackenzie had walked over to them, curious as to what they had been talking about exactly.

"Well?" they asked, tapping their toe impatiently.

"Miles asked if he would like us to stay at their village since the castle is now gone," Ronan replied.

"The village, that's still around?"

Miles nodded.

"Do you remember Richard? he's still there. He's the one who's been looking after everything, while we've been over here."

"Really? that's good to hear. When are we going to be heading over?" Mackenzie asked.

5

"Honestly? we should be heading there tonight since we don't exactly have a home now," Ronan said.

"Alright, let's just wait for Xavier. He should be finished telling the others soon," Miles said.

A few minutes later, Xavier had returned from telling the others of their new living arrangements.

"Thanks, Uncle Xavier, we're leaving tonight. Is that okay with you?" Ronan asked.

"Fine by me, should we get going?" Xavier replied.

Turning towards where Theo was, Ronan called for him to come over.

"Theo, can you come here for a second?" he asked.

"You called Ronan?" Theo said, speeding over to them.

"Can you do me a favour?"

"Of course, anything."

"Miles invited us to his camp and I was wondering could you shift and walk with me and Xavier, just to keep everyone safe?"

"Of course, I will."

Shirking off his clothes, Theo quickly turned until a large black wolf that had luminous blue eyes stood in his place. Giving his head a brief shake, he gazed up at Ronan and Xavier.

"Let's go, guys. Will you be walking with us, Miles?" Ronan asked.

"I'd like to," Miles replied.

"Alright, let's get going."

Their group walked down the streets until they stood at the city's harbor with Ronan, Miles, Xavier, Mackenzie, and Theo at the front.

Miles looked around quickly to make sure that no one was watching them. Once he saw the coast was clear, he ran over to a large white wooden shed that looked decrepit on the outside. Forcing the door open, he walked in and found a few boats, walking past them he opened a large corrugated door that was the former owners used when using the boats. He made sure to be careful when pushing out them out because he didn't want to make any unnecessary noise. Once the boats were ready, Miles crept out of the shed and called over the others.

"Let's go, guys, quickly. We have to hurry!" he whispered, anxiously.

"Hey, get back here!" a voice yelled from behind where the group was.

Miles whipped his head in the direction of the yelling and saw that running towards them was a few of the young men from earlier. Miles began to quickly usher all of them passed the shed and into the boats. As they were getting on the boats, Mackenzie nearly got grabbed but thankfully didn't because Cole grabbed them first. Theo shifted back once they were on the water and carefully made his way towards where Ronan sat on the boat.

"What are you thinking?" Theo asked him.

"We need to get back at whoever burned down the castle," Ronan said, slowly.

"Do you think you know who did it?" Theo asked, in surprise. "I have some guesses. Don't you think it was odd that when we came across that group, something always happened?" Ronan asked.

Thinking, Theo's eyes widened in realization.

"I think you're right, Ronan. So, what do you consider we do then?"

"Once we get settled, I'd like us to talk to Miles about what we could possibly do."

"Alright."

About 20 minutes later, they reached the island's shore. Waiting for them on the shore, was Richard the island's entrance keeper. He was a tall, thin, middle-aged, greying-hair man who had deep forest-green eyes.

"Welcome!" he greeted them as they passed him on their boats.

Once they reached the shore, everyone got out of the boats and they walked into the village. The village was gorgeous, Ronan noticed as he walked into it, that they had built houses during their time there clearly establishing a community.

"Most of those houses are unoccupied so pick whichever one you'd like. I'll be by later to check in on you guys," Miles said.

Going their separate ways, Ronan, Theo, and Mackenzie chose to share one of the small bungalows. The house they had ended up choosing had a lovely beige roof with the rest of its exterior being painted a soft peach colour, it had a red door and window frames to finish off the look.

Entering the house, they immediately walked into the living room which had the sofa placed against the wall, near the window and opposite that was a 50-inch television; also, in the living room, beside each side of the sofa was a tablet. Heading upstairs, the three of them got their first look at their bedrooms.

Their bedrooms which were on the above floor, each had a different paint job which was the only difference of the room. Otherwise, the room had a double sized bed that was against the same wall that the bedroom door was. Near the headboard was a bedside table, that had a small lamp and a box of Kleenex and opposite that was a decently-sized deep oak desk with a chair to match.

In Ronan's room specifically, he had placed the duffel bag that he always carried around with him on the floor. Opening it, he removed what few possessions he had in it and placed them carefully on the bedside table. Once he was settled, Ronan left his room and headed downstairs. Situated at the table and about to eat, they heard a knock at the door. Walking over to it, Mackenzie opened it revealing Miles standing on the porch.

"Hey Miles, this place is amazing. It's just so beautiful," Theo said from his spot in the entrance way.

"Would you like to come in?" Ronan asked.

Miles shook his head.

"I wanted to let you guys know that we made dinner since we figured you would appreciate a nice hot meal," he said.

Smiling, they nodded.

"We'd love to," Ronan replied.

"Great, see you in a bit," Miles said, smiling. He stepped back and opened the door and left soon after.

When Miles was out the door, Ronan turned towards Theo and Mackenzie.

"Are you guys settled? I'd like to go get some dinner," he said.

"Yeah, we're ready when you are," Mackenzie said.

Grabbing their jackets, the three of them left the house and headed back to the village's pit.

When they reached the pit, they saw people dancing around the firepit and food was laid out before them. They walked towards them and specifically towards Miles.

"Hey guys, Welcome! Grab some food and enjoy yourselves," Miles said.

"Thank you, Miles," said Theo.

They walked to where the food was and grabbed a plate. The three of them chose a little of everything to put on their plate. The ladies who had prepared the meal had made a delicious roast beef and potatoes that was all covered in gravy.

"This is delicious!" Mackenzie exclaimed.

"Agreed," Theo said.

As they were eating, a young man walked towards them.
"Mac is that you?" he said.

"Alexander, you're still alive?" Mackenzie asked.

"I can't believe that you're still alive."

"Yeah, I am. Ronan's father and his friends found hiding out at Sick Kids Hospital."

"Really?"

"Yeah, they've looked after me since. So, what's new with you?"

"Do you remember Marissa?"
"Of course. That girl that you used to hang around all the time?" "Yeah! We got married and now she's expecting our first son," he said, with a smile.

"Really? that's great news. Congratulations!"

"Thank you. We're really excited," Alexander said.

"I can imagine. I'm really happy for both of you."

"So, is there anyone that I should know about?" he teased, a playful smirk curled on his lips.

"Well, I do have someone who misses me back in Vancouver."

"Really? I hope he's treating you well," Alexander said.

"Who is?" a voice said, approaching them.

Mackenzie turned slightly and smiled.

"Matteo," they replied.

"My cousin?" Theo asked, he came around and took a seat beside Mackenzie.

"Alexander was just asking me about him."

"Oh okay. I'm Theo, by the way. It's nice to meet you," Theo said, extending a hand.

Alexander quickly took the offered hand and shook it.

"Likewise, I'm Alexander."

"So, you've known Mackenzie a long time?"

"I have. We basically grew up together."

Just then, they heard someone clearing their throat. Ronan appeared to have had moved to where he thought he'd be heard the best when speaking.

"May I have your attention?" he called from his spot in front.

Noticing where Ronan had taken up and that he was about to speak, everyone had stopped what they were doing and turned to face where he stood.

"Something happened while he crossed the lake and we nearly got captured by a group of the same men. We need to do something. I've spoken to Miles and he agrees with me that we need to get prepared should we get attacked," he said, "so, starting tomorrow we will be working on strengthening whatever aspects we need to, so you'll have to turn in early tonight. Thank you for listening and I'll see you all early tomorrow."

Ronan stepped away and walked back towards where his friends stood. They walked towards their home and went to bed, turning in for the night.

# CHAPTER SEVEN

The following morning, Ronan awoke and headed to Miles' place. He wanted to speak with him about what they could do about Dylan and the now newly re-formed Sanguists. He turned to Theo who had come with him, his expression, serious.

"Could you grab Xavier? We need to meet at Miles' place," Ronan said to Theo.

When Theo quickly ran off, Ronan headed straight towards Miles' house where he'd meet up with the others. Arriving at his house a few minutes later, Ronan was pleased when he saw that Miles hadn't left yet.

"Great. You're just the person I wanted to see," he said to him.

"Of course. How can I help?" Miles asked.

Just then, Theo ran up to them and was closely followed by Xavier. "Oh good, I'm glad we caught you," Theo said.
"Oh, now I'm interested in why. Would you like to come in?" Miles asked.

The three of them nodded entering Miles' home. When they had gone in, they saw just how lovely and quaint his home really was, Miles was an orderly person and his home really showed that.

"So, what happened?"

"Just as we were headed back here we nearly got caught by a group of guys in some dark hoods," said Ronan.

"You guys nearly got caught by a group of Sanguists?" Miles asked in alarm.

"The Sanguists are still around?" Ronan asked.

Miles nodded.

"I think they laid low for a while after Damien was killed. It seems like now they've regrouped, and have a new leader," he said.

Just then, they were interrupted by a knock at the door. Walking over to it, Theo opened it revealing Xavier standing on Miles' porch.

"Hey Xavier, come on in. I was just telling Miles what happened just as we were coming over," Theo said to him as he allowed him to enter. "What do you think Miles?" Xavier asked, walking over to the others and took a seat.

"From what they told me I think that you guys ran into some Sanguists," Miles said.

"Really?" Xavier said.

Miles nodded.

Xavier turned towards Ronan, gazing at him, curiously.

"What are we going to do?" he asked Ronan.

Ronan opened his mouth, just about to answer when they heard a loud bang coming from just outside Miles' door. Rushing outside, what they saw looked like something straight out of a nightmare, people were screaming or now laid murdered; somehow the Sanguists had gotten on to the island.

Miles looked around in anguish, everything had been trashed. He had walked over to one of the houses where a message had been smeared. "Hey Ronan, can you come over here please?" he asked in barely concealed anger.

Wondering why Miles was so clearly angry, Ronan walked over to him, confused.

"What is it?" he asked.

"Have a look," Miles said, shortly.

Curiously, Ronan turned and looked at the outside of the house where a note had been messily written.

*Your Majesty,*

*I was really looking forward to meeting you today, unfortunately, when I stopped by to visit you didn't seem to be there, so I decided to leave this thoughtful message.*

*-   D*

"How did they get onto here? I mean isn't Richard usually pretty strict on who can come over here?" Theo asked.

Eyes widening, Miles' head whipped around, his eyes meeting Theo's.

"Oh my God, Richard!" he exclaimed.

He ran back towards the island's shoreline and dropped to his knees once he found him. Richard lay by the shore, his eyes wide and unseeing, and chest viciously was torn into.

"Oh, my old friend what have they done to you?" Miles cried, anguished, holding Richard's body in his arms. The others ran over to where Miles was and knelt by his side.

"That bastard killed Richard, he killed him!" Miles cried out, tears had begun to fall down his cheeks. Mackenzie came beside him and placed a hand on Miles' shoulder, consolingly. Slowly he raised his head and looked at them, desolately.

"I think I know who it is," Mackenzie said.

"Are you sure?" Miles asked, surprised.

They nodded.

"When we went into the city, we came across a group of young men and my brother, Chase was among them."

"Chase is alive?" Miles asked in disbelief.

"Yeah. He's been staying with a man named Dylan who convinced him he's helping him."

"What?"

"Yeah, it's only after I'd gotten through to him that he seemed to change his mind," they said.

"Yeah," Mackenzie said.

"I'm just glad that he's alright."

"Me too."

"Hey guys, not to cut this short, but what are we going to do about Dylan?" Ronan asked.

Miles wiped at his eyes and got to his feet.

"You're right. What do you think we should do?" he asked.

"We need to work on strengthening certain concepts. So maybe we should concentrate on that for now," Ronan said.

1

"Alright, in the meantime we should really give everyone a proper burial," Miles said.

Everyone nodded and headed back into the village, Theo had decided to shift, and they placed Richard's body onto his back so that he could carry him into the village.

When they reached the village, Miles gently removed Richard's body off of Theo's back and onto the ground until they could bury him. Ronan ran off in search of a shovel, which he quickly found. When he returned he was horrified to find that Mackenzie and Miles were being held hostage while Theo watched on warily, frozen in place.

"Oh good, your majesty. Lovely of you to join us," said one of the young men, who was holding Mackenzie hostage.

"Let Mackenzie go!" Ronan yelled.

"Of course, if you do as I say."

"Who are you?"

"You surely read the note I left behind?" the young man asked.

"That was you?" Ronan said.

"Certainly. What did you think?" Dylan asked.

I did. Nothing but the ramblings of a madman I'm sure. What is that you want?"

"I thought my note was clear, I want to finish what he started."

"Who?"

"The rightful king."

"My uncle, surely you can't be serious?"

"Deadly. Oh, and don't follow us back to the mainland or we'll kill all of you if you do. Make no mistake," he said, dropping Mackenzie roughly, he and the others who had made to leave, turned back momentarily.

They stood stock still as Dylan and his men moved quickly towards the shore and got back into the boat that they'd come to the island in. Once he was sure that Dylan had left, Ronan helped everyone who had survived up to their feet.

◆◆◆

About a month later, Chase dropped by for the first time. He had agreed to meet Mackenzie at the shoreline so that he could be led into the village. Mackenzie was at the shoreline when they saw a small blue sailboat coming towards them. Once his boat reached the island's shoreline, Mackenzie ran down and met him there.

"Welcome Chase!" they shouted when they reached Chase's boat.

Chase tied off his boat and carefully got out. Once he did, he grabbed a small brown leather bag that was in it and walked over to Mackenzie, smiling.

"Hey Mac, shall we go in?"

"Yeah, c'mon."

Chase wrapped an around their shoulders and Mackenzie led him into the village. As they were heading in, Chase got tackled to the ground by Theo who picked up roughly and held him up tightly by the scruff of his neck.

"Who are you, what do you want here?" he asked, his face mere inches from Chase's, his eyes narrowed in suspicion.

"Wait, Theo, he's my brother!" Mackenzie yelled, coming closer.

"You know this guy?" he asked them.

"Yes, I do."

After a few minutes of scrutiny, Theo let Chase go and brushed his shoulders off.

"Sorry about that, we just had someone attack our village and everyone's been more on high alert lately," said Theo.

"I know. I'm sorry about all that," Chase said.

"Why? It wasn't your fault. Come on, we'll get you some food and you can come and meet everyone."

As they were walking in, Chase froze in his tracks. Standing mere feet from him was Miles who had a shocked lock on his face.

7

"Chase is that really you?" he asked, softly.

Breaking off at a run, Chase nearly tackled Miles to the ground. Laughing, he helped Chase to his feet and brushed his shoulders off.

"It's so good to see you, Miles," Chase said, with a smile on his lips and an amused look in his eyes.

"Likewise. Come on, let's get you fed," Miles said, smiling.

He, Chase, and, Mackenzie walked into the village and into where the kitchens were. To their surprise, the two of them found Ronan already there.

"Oh! Who's this?" Ronan asked.

Sticking out a hand to shake, Chase smiled.

"Hi I'm Chase, Mackenzie's brother," he said.

Taking it and shaking it, Ronan grinned.

"It's nice to meet you, Chase. I didn't know you had a brother, Mackenzie," Ronan said.

"I didn't mention him before because I thought that I had lost him. We got separated when we were kids," Mackenzie explained.

"Well, it's nice to have you back among us," Theo said.

"Thanks, everyone, I appreciate the warm reception. Even if it's at a risk," Chase said.

"What risk?" Ronan asked.

"Didn't Mackenzie tell you about Dylan and what he did to me?"

"What? No, they didn't," Theo replied, shocked.

"Shortly after Mackenzie and I were separated, he found me and took me in, and from what I understand, brainwashed me to be his perfect little soldier."

"Are you here to spy on us for your master, then?" Ronan asked, accusingly.

"No! believe me, I'm hurt the fact that he lied to me. I really thought Mackenzie was dead," Chase explained.

"Really?"

"Of course! I love Mackenzie, why would I ever be intentionally away from them?"

"I'm sorry. You're right, of course, you wouldn't do that," said Ronan.

"Don't worry about it. Now, what's for lunch?" Chase asked.

"I was just about to make sandwiches. Would you like one?"

Chase nodded.

"Sure, what are the ingredients?" he asked.

"I took out some cheese, cold cuts, lettuce, and a couple of other things," Theo said.

"Sounds good, pass the bread?" Chase asked.

Grabbing the bag of bread, Ronan passed it to Chase who took it and opened it. Taking out two slices of it, he passed the bag to his sibling who took some for themselves. Ronan and Theo did the same as well and ended up making five separate types of sandwiches.

◆◆◆

When they finished, Miles took the plates and placed all of them into the sink. Then he turned back towards the others, his back resting against the edge of the sink with his arms crossed as he watched the others finish up.

"Would you guys want to watch a film until Chase has to head back?" he asked.

"Sure," Mackenzie replied.

"Of course," Theo said.

"I'd like to, thank you," Chase said.

Straightening up, Miles uncrossed his arms and walked towards the entrance.

"I'll be right back, guys. I'm going to grab the film player and I'm going to see if I can find some movies to watch."

He finally left the room and the others were left to talk among one another. Chase spent the next little while of what we could learning about Mackenzie and what he'd missed.

Half an hour, Theo returned with a small rectangular box and put onto the table for just a moment. Then he walked over to the far-right wall and grabbed the TV that was there and brought it over. Walking back over to the table, he grabbed the player and walked over to the TV and hooked it up. He then opened the player and placed the movie in it and started it. The movie that Miles had picked was an action/adventure movie that had made them laugh while watching it.

Finally, after an hour later, the movie had finished, and they hurried to get Chase to the shore so that he could get back before he was missed by anyone.

When they reached the shore, Chase opened the bag he had brought with him and removed the robes that he kept there and slipped them on. He then turned towards Mackenzie and pulled them into a hug.

"I'll miss you, Mac. See you in a month," he said.

Saying goodbye, Chase adjusted his bag and got into the boat that he came in. He unraveled the sail of the boat and got into it, he then pushed off the shore and made his way across the water and back to his camp.

Watching him leave, Mackenzie turned towards the others after Chase was out of sight.

"Today was a good day, but we should get some rest. I'm sure you guys are all exhausted from today," they said.

Wishing each other goodnight, Mackenzie, Ronan, and, Theo headed back to their place while Miles headed back to his and turned in for that night.

1

Nancy A. Lopes

# CHAPTER EIGHT

Over the course of the next few months, Chase's face had quickly become a familiar and welcome face among those at the village, everyone seemed to like him very much. One day, as Theo was by the pit doing a few tasks Chase had arrived by boat and upon reaching the village, collapsed onto the ground. Getting to his feet, Theo rushed over to him, quickly and attempted to revive him.

"Chase are you okay?" he asked, frantically.

Not getting a response, Theo gathered Chase into his arms and broke off at a run until he reached the infirmary. Entering it, he found to his relief, one of the nurses there waiting, patiently.

"Hi, can you take care of my friend's brother?" Theo asked, timidly as he shifted Chase in his arms.

3

"Of course. Place him down on one of the beds," the woman said.

Shifting him around slightly, Theo placed Chase onto one of the beds. He turned towards the woman, gratefully.

"Thank you so much. I'm Theo, it's nice to meet you," he said.

"I'm Laura, it's nice to meet you, what's his name?" she asked Theo, nodding towards Chase.

"His name is Chase, I don't know what's wrong with him. He just collapsed when he arrived here by boat so that he could visit Mackenzie," Theo's eyes widened as if realizing something, "I have to get Mackenzie! Can you stay with him for a few minutes while I get them?" he asked.

"Certainly," she replied.

"Thank you so much. I'll be right back," he said, grabbing his jacket and hurried over to the door so that he could find Mackenzie.

Meanwhile, back at the infirmary, Laura had begun preparations on how she could treat Chase. Looking him over, she found a series of cuts and scratches all over his body, she also found that his leg had been broken as well.

Walking over to the sink, which was against the left wall of the room she bent down and reached under it, pulling out a small pewter bowl from it, she then filled it and brought it over to where Chase was. When the bowl was placed down, she moved to grab some bandages that were in one of the cupboards and brought them to where the bowl was. Taking out the rag that was in the bowl, Laura began to gently cleanse Chase's injuries, she then moved onto covering them and bandaged his leg up. Just as she was finishing up, Theo rushed in with Mackenzie on his heels.

"Where the hell is my brother!" Mackenzie yelled.

Following Mackenzie, Theo placed his hands gently on their shoulders.

"Calm down. He's laying over there," he replied, gesturing towards where Chase now lay, unconscious.

They ran over to his bed and looked him over, frantically seeing the bandages and the cast on his leg.

"What happened?" they asked, looking up at Theo in alarm.

"I don't know, he collapsed as soon as he arrived here. I guess we'll know is when he finally wakes up."

"Yeah, I suppose so."

8

One day as Mackenzie was sitting with Chase, Cole walked in.

"Hey Cole, what brings you here?" they asked, eyebrows raised.

"Dad told me what happened," Cole replied.

"Theo told him?"

Cole nodded.

"Yeah, I'm glad he did. I wanted to check in on you," he said.

"That's sweet of you, Cole. Thank you, would you like to sit with me?"

"Sure, that would be nice."

They had been speaking to one another for a while when suddenly to their shock and horror, Chase stiffened and began to convulse violently.

"Quick! Help me lower him back down onto the bed," Mackenzie shouted, as they moved to Chase's right side. The two of them each grabbed a side and they lowered his body down, very gently. When they had, Mackenzie turned back towards Cole, anxiously.

"Cole, do me a favour and grab a bowl and fill it with it," they said, raising a hand, Mackenzie placed it gently upon Chase's forehead, "damn, he's developing a fever."

Quickly getting to his feet, Cole raised a hand and swept it through his hair. He then anxiously ran his hands over the span of his waistcoat and then quickly moved over towards the sink. Taking a deep breath, Cole grabbed the bowl that was in the sink and filled it, placing one of the rags that was near it into the bowl. Once the bowl was filled, Cole brought it over and Mackenzie took it from him.

Placing the bowl down, Mackenzie reached into the bowl and took out the rag and squeezed all the water out of it and placed it on Chase's forehead. For the next while, both Mackenzie and Cole sat with Chase until he hopefully awoke.

Six hours later, they heard a rustling sound coming from where Chase had been laying. When they turned around, they saw to their absolute elation that he had regained consciousness.

"Chase, you're awake. Thank goodness!" Mackenzie exclaimed, running over to the right side of where he lay.

"What happened?" he asked, clutching at his forehead, groaning.

"You don't remember?"

Chase shook his head, confused.

"All I remember is passing out twice."

"You passed out twice? I guess I must have found you the second time when you got to the island," Theo said.

"Yeah, I suppose."

"Do you remember who knocked you out the first time?" Mackenzie asked.

"Not really but I may have a guess. All the times that I came here, someone from my camp must have follow me and eventually knocked me out when I came here to visit," Chase explained.

"Mackenzie can you stay with Chase?" Theo asked, getting to his feet and pulled on his jacket.

"Of course, what are you thinking?" Mackenzie asked.

"Just a few quick things that I need to do. Can I get you guys anything to eat?" he asked.

"Sure, I'm kind of hungry. How about you?" Mackenzie asked Chase.

"Yeah, me too," he replied, as his stomach growled.

"Okay, I guess I'll be back soon then," Theo replied, leaving the infirmary.

Chase and Mackenzie had been speaking to one another for well over an hour when suddenly, the door to the infirmary was opened with a loud bang. Alarmed, Mackenzie turned sharply in their seat, wonder- ing who had entered so abruptly.

"Where is he, Where's Chase?" Miles asked.

"Miles?" Chase's voice asked from where he had been laying the entire time.

Turning sharply, Miles' eyes landed on him.

"Chase, you recognize me?" Miles croaked out.

Chase nodded.

"Yeah, I think I do," he replied, slowly.

"Really?"

"Yeah."

Throwing his arms around Miles' neck, Chase pulled him into a tight hug, as he began to sob.

"It's so good to see you, Miles," he said, once he'd finished wiping the tears from his eyes.

"Likewise, I'm glad that you're back," said Miles.

Theo walked in several minutes later, his arms filled with containers of food. Walking over, he placed everything down, making sure to not spill any of it. Once he had, he took a seat and took a deep breath.

"I got a little of everything, guys. Ronan should be here very soon, he said he wanted to be updated."

"Alright, that's good," Mackenzie replied.

Chase reached over to the containers and opened one and began to eat a tuna pasta that was lightly drizzled with some mayonnaise. Meanwhile, Mackenzie had grabbed another tupperware that had an egg salad that had a few drops of blood in it. Just as they were finishing up, Ronan walked in, looking relieved.

"Hey Chase, so good to see you're alright. Do you know what happened?" he asked.

"I have a guess. I think all the times that I came to visit, Dylan had me followed and today I got knocked out," Chase replied.

"We need to do something. He killed Richard and now he hurt Chase, he needs to be stopped before he hurts anyone else."

"You're right. We need to take a stand," Theo said.

"What do you propose we do, Ronan?" Miles asked.

"I want to get everyone trained and ready," Ronan said.

"Alright, sounds good," Theo replied.

"Since almost everyone is immortal, except for a few humans I think an obstacle course is the best way to go about doing this."

"When do you want to do this?" Theo asked.

"In a few days, it'll be the start of the month and we can work through it for that entire month," Ronan said.

"Okay. I'll tell my group what we have planned," said Miles.

"Alright, sounds good," said Ronan.

A few days later, they awoke bright and early and headed to the pit where they found Miles waiting for them, appearing to be excited about what they were about to do.

"Good Morning Everyone! I hope you all slept well. Today we'll be going to a secluded location and working through an obstacle course.
Now if you'd follow me I'd like to show you where we'll be practicing," he said.

Miles jumped off the stage and looked over his shoulder as the others followed him closely.

The obstacle course was huge. They'd start with a single hurdle, jumping on a pull-up bar they would do about five pull-ups and then jump off. Afterward, they would climb up another rope again and move down a zipline, after which they would climb a massive wall and then would climb a rope, touching the top bar that the rope was attached to. Finally, they would then scurry down the rope, finishing the course. Ronan had everyone split up into groups of four; each of those groups were required to go through the course in under 10-15 minutes. Those that failed to do so, had to complete the course again.

9

"I want everyone to line up. On my whistle, you will move throughout the course. And…go!"

He raised the whistle to his lips and blew on it, signaling the start for the first group to begin. They broke off at a run and moved swiftly through the course. The only group that completed the course just shortly after then was the group that had Mackenzie in it and that was because they were the only one who wasn't a mortal.

Finally, at the end of the day, their group headed back to the village, waiting for them when they arrived, was a delicious array of food in the kitchen. Grabbing a few plates that were stocked there, they began to fill them with the food that had been spread out for them. After they had eaten, Mackenzie, Ronan, and, Theo got to their feet and walked over to Miles.

"We're going to head to bed. We'll see you tomorrow," Ronan said, smiling.

"Alright, see you guys tomorrow," Miles replied.

A few minutes later, the three of them arrived back at their home and got ready for bed. They said goodnight to one another and promptly went to bed.

The following morning, Mackenzie awoke and walked deliriously into the kitchen where they began to make themselves a cup of coffee. After they had their breakfast in hand, Mackenzie went on a search for Theo. Finding him, several minutes later having a sparring match with Miles they decided to watch them fight for a bit, taking a seat. They had been locked in a bout when Mackenzie had arrived, for a while, they surveyed one another until Theo smirked and lunged forward using only a bit of his strength to tackle Miles.

"Is that all you've got?" Miles asked, with a laugh from under Theo's boot.

Theo shook his head, chuckling.

"Is that better?" he asked.

Rolling his eyes, he grinned.

"Help me up, will you?" he asked.

Chuckling, Theo stuck out a hand and helped Miles to his feet. Just then, Laura rushed over to where they were, anxiously.

"Miles, you have to come quick, it's Chase, he's gone!" she exclaimed.

"How, did you see who took him?" he asked.

Laura shook her head.

"No, I didn't."

Growing frustrated, Miles stormed into the village and went up to different people and began to ask them if they had seen Chase, which unfortunately they hadn't. Finally, when it seemed that everything felt hopeless, someone spoke up.

"I may have seen something," a young man with short light brown hair and blue-green eyes said.

Miles turned around, his gaze suspicious.

"Oh, what did you see?" he asked.

"Um, well…there was this guy who showed up and said that he wanted to see Chase," the young man explained.

"You let a complete stranger go into the infirmary?"

The young man nodded slowly.

"I didn't think there was anything wrong with it," he said, with a shrug.
"Nothing wrong? You let someone who you didn't know who basically kidnap one of the people here," Miles said, "did you at least get his name?"

The young man nodded.

"He told me his name was Dylan."

Nancy A. Lopes

# CHAPTER NINE

$Y$ou let the man who killed most of the people who were living here into the village?" Ronan asked, furiously.

"Yes," the young man asked, nervously.

"How could you be so irresponsible and stupid? He could have come in and decided to finish what he had started, you're very lucky that he didn't!"

"I know, sir. I'm sorry. It won't happen again."

"It had better not."

Miles turned towards the others.

"Alright, we need to get Chase back. Do we have any idea where his camp may be?" he asked.

9

Everyone shook their head except for Theo who appeared to be in thought. Finally, a few minutes later, he realized something.

"Hey Ronan, where did Damien have his camp, do you remember?" Theo asked.

Ronan nodded slowly, thinking carefully.

"I think so. If I remember correctly, it wasn't that far from where my father had our castle built right before the uprising took place. Wait do you think that's where Dylan's camp may be?" he asked.

"Yeah, probably."

In that case, we should hurry before Dylan does anymore serious harm to Chase," Miles replied.

"Definitely, I'll round up my group and you should gather yours," Ronan said.

"When do you want to head out?"

"Give me a few minutes and then we can go. We'll need to take the boats in order to reach the mainland."

◆◆◆

About an hour later, both of their groups were on a couple of boats and headed for the shore of the mainland. The weather that evening caused small waves to appear onto the lake's surface.

They got to the shoreline about 15 minutes later with everyone who had come with all in one piece. Getting out of the boats, they began to make their way throughout the city and slowly towards the camp. It had turned out that Dylan's camp really wasn't that far from Damien's former grounds. Ronan thought as they walked through the streets, that it was pretty strange that for a man claiming to be "Jackson's son", he seemed awfully stuck with this crazy story that somehow, he was "his son", when he's certain Jackson never fathered any children, given his age at the time.

Finally reaching the building that Dylan had chosen, they noticed that it was a large, rundown, decrepit-looking building that had been broken into a couple of times.

1

Walking in, Ronan, Mackenzie, Miles and, Theo began to look around the main atrium. Exchanging glances, they knew that they had to be careful when moving through the eerily quiet vacant halls. Ronan remained suspicious through the entire time which turned out to be proven right when they came across two young men draped in those familiar dark robes.

"Keep running. I'll catch up," Theo said, shooting Ronan and Miles a sharp look.

When they ran off, Theo shifted and stood before the two as a wolf, growly lowly. He continued to stand that way until one of them, a young tanned man with light brown eyes and short wavy light brown hair moved closer as if to grab him. Theo lunged forward and managed to mildly injure the first and severely injure the second when they tried to hurt him in turn. Once he was sure they weren't going to follow him, Theo ran off and shifted only when he was sure that he was out of earshot of the two boys.

Meanwhile, the others were two floors above where had left Theo. All of a sudden, as they were moving throughout the halls they heard two very distinct voices coming from behind one of the doors.

"Master, what's going on?" the younger of the two voices asked from behind closed doors.

"Hush child. Remember what I told you, you must remain quiet," the other voice replied, a clearly older voice than the first.

"That's Chase!" Mackenzie exclaimed, in a whisper.

"Are you sure?" Ronan asked.

They nodded.

"I recognize my brother's voice anywhere."

"So that must mean the other voice is Dylan's then," Theo replied, looking between both Mackenzie and Ronan.

"Must be. And if that's the case? Then we need to be very careful because if they're together, something's changed," Ronan replied. "How are we going to do this?" Theo asked.

Thinking carefully for a few minutes, Ronan's eyes widened as he realized something.

1

"Wait for my signal," was all he said, as Theo and Mackenzie exchanged glances with Ronan.

Nodding, they watched as Ronan intently watched the doors for the next little while, which they continued to do until the moment he finally got his chance.

Slowly straightening up, an excited look appeared on Ronan's face. Seeing Ronan's stance change, Mackenzie, Miles and, Theo exchanged glances with one another. Miles looked over at the others indicating that Ronan had given his signal.

Once the coast was clear, they once again moved until they were standing in front of the doors where Dylan and Chase's voices were coming from. Taking a hold of the doorknob, Ronan quietly opened the door and carefully walked into the room, the others following closely behind. He soon found himself at a loss of what he saw; Dylan was watching them as Chase was kept close.

# CHAPTER TEN

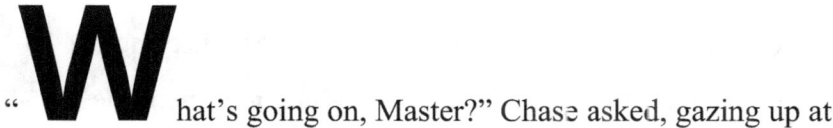

"What's going on, Master?" Chase asked, gazing up at

Dylan in anxious confusion.

"Don't worry, I won't let them hurt you," he cooed, bringing him closer.

"Hurt him? You kidnapped him from us!" Mackenzie yelled.

Looking back at Dylan, Chase bit his lip in confusion.

"Is what they're saying true, why do they look so familiar?" Chase asked, pointing at Mackenzie.

1

"They're lying. Don't you remember what I told you? They kidnapped you," Dylan replied.

"No, we didn't! Chase you're my brother. I looked everywhere for you, every day. Don't you remember Miles taking the both of us in and raising us after mom died?" Mackenzie asked.

Chase frowned, slightly as he thought over what Mackenzie had told him. He found himself torn about what Dylan had been saying and now what Mackenzie had told him. It didn't help that now he was being bombarded by a colossal onslaught of what were memories that he was trying to make sense of. He clutched at his head as the onslaught of memories continued, finally after a while, Chase dropped his hands from his head and looked over at Mackenzie again. As he took in their features, Chase found himself realizing who they were.

His jaw dropped as he got to his feet and closely walked over to Mackenzie, tears filling his eyes.

"Mac? I'm so sorry. I shouldn't have believed what he told me," he croaked out.

Pulling him closer, Mackenzie hugged him desperately trying to calm him down.

"Shh.. shh.. it's okay. I don't blame you for what's happened you were being brainwashed," they replied, "I'm just glad that you're safe, Chase."

As they were speaking, Dylan who had watched everything in an escalating rage, got to his feet and sped over to where Chase and Mackenzie were. Coming from behind Chase, Dylan shot a hand that went through Chase's chest. He went pulled it back out, just as sharply. Mackenzie screamed as they caught Chase as he collapsed into their arms. Rushing over, Ronan took a hold of Mackenzie's sleeve and turned them to face him.

"Mac, you need to listen to me. I can save your brother, but you need to listen," he explained.

Mackenzie turned towards Ronan, appearing lost but with traces of hope swimming in their eyes. He noticed that their face was red and that they had tears streaked down their cheeks.

"Y-you can help?"

Ronan nodded.

1

"How?"

"I'm going to have to turn him," he said, gently.

"But, why?"

"Because that's the only way that Chase can be saved, Mackenzie."

"Okay," they replied, carefully handing over Chase's now broken body.

Taking him from Mackenzie's arms, Ronan laid him down gently and took a glance at Chase, he then turned towards them.

"Could you please prop his head up, Mackenzie?" he asked them.

Nodding, they gently took a hold of Chase's head and raised it just a bit. Once they did, Ronan took a brief glance around the both of them, making sure that everything was safe. Once he deemed everything safe, Ronan raised his wrist up to his lips and extended the sharp row of teeth that lay just behind his original set. He lowered his head and sank them into the flesh of his wrist. Once he'd done so, he brought it just over Chase's mouth and let his blood drip into it. Once he finished doing so, Ronan pulled back his wrist and watched Chase closely as knit itself back up again.

◆◆◆

Finally, a few minutes later, Chase slowly opened his eyes and made to sit up. Noticing what he was about to do, Mackenzie gently took a hold of his shoulders and lightly pushed him down again. Confused as to who was touching his shoulders, he turned his head and was met by Mackenzie's reassured gaze.

"What happened?" he asked them, his gaze curious.

"We thought we lost you Chase. Dylan nearly killed you, if it wasn't for Ronan turning you, you wouldn't have made it," Mackenzie explained.

"Ronan turned me?" Chase asked, realization dawning on his face, "that's why everything feels as different as it does."

Mackenzie nodded.

"Thank you, Ronan. I really appreciate it," he said, meeting Ronan's eyes.

"My pleasure," Ronan replied.

1

"Hmm…maybe you aren't as useless as I thought," a voice mused from behind them.

Getting to his feet, Cole who had overheard Dylan's words turned slowly and saw him standing behind him, arms crossed and a smug smirk on his lips.

"What did you just say?" Cole asked.

"The boy? Oh yeah, I was just going to do away with him once I no longer had a use for him."

"How dare you, he idolized and cared about you!"

"Did he? Well that's his fault not mine. To tell you the truth, he was really weak and small."

Enraged, Cole flexed his neck from side to side and in doing so, extended his razor-sharp canines that lay just behind his mortal teeth.
Lunging forward, Cole went for his throat; which he side-stepped.

"Is that all you've got?" he asked with a laugh, as he watched Cole scramble to his feet.

"I haven't even started," Cole replied.

Razor sharp teeth still extended, he lowered himself into a crouch and began to survey him carefully. He was considering exactly how he should act, he needed to be careful since Dylan was unpredictable.

"Are you gonna stay there all day?" he asked, irritated.

Shooting Dylan a brief smirk, they continued to survey one another until finally Cole saw his shot and got to his feet and leapt forward intending to once again go for his throat.

Just when he thought he'd successfully caught a hold of his throat, Dylan grabbed Cole and pulled him into a chokehold. Locking eyes with Mackenzie, he smirked briefly, his grip tightened on Cole's neck. He twisted his neck, breaking it and killed him almost instantly.

◆◆◆

Once he was done, Dylan dropped him unceremoniously and broke off at a run, attempting to get away. Seeing what had happened, Mackenzie,

1

Xavier and, Theo quickly both joined Cole's side and desperately tried to revive him. When they failed though, Mackenzie collapsed on Cole's body, and sobbed.

Seeing a small group gathered that looked upset, Ronan ran over to them, curious as to what had happened. He felt his blood run cold and his heart pumping in his ears when he saw his son's prone body strewn awkwardly on the corner of the street.

"What happened?" Ronan demanded, his voice breaking slightly at the end.

He knelt down to where his son now lay and gathered him into my arms. Tears began to stream down his face as anger, confusion, loss tore through him.

"It was Dylan," Mackenzie explained, watching as Ronan took the utmost care when tending to his son's body, "he and Cole had been fighting when suddenly Dylan grabbed him and got him into a chokehold. After that he just snapped his neck."

As he processed Mackenzie's words, Ronan began to feel a slow burning rage fill him. He would get his revenge but first he had to find Dylan.

"Did you see where he ran off to?" he asked Mackenzie, turning towards them.

Mackenzie pointed towards where the doors were. Leaving them behind, Ronan got to his feet and ran off hoping to get his chance at revenge for his son's murder. He ran down the halls and was soon past the doors and searched the abandoned streets for Dylan.

Spotting him, Ronan tried to catch up with him and when he couldn't, shouted out to him.

"Hey!"

Hearing Ronan's voice, Dylan stopped and turned, his face had a look of cruel amusement.

"Come to avenge your little boy?" he sneered.

"How dare you kill my son!"

"Killing your son was simple. He didn't put up that much of a fight, to be honest. What a weakling."

1

"Don't you dare call him a weakling. You don't have the right!" "Perhaps now you'll give me what I want. You know, I fully intend on continuing what my father couldn't and exterminate all those who aren't worthy," Dylan yelled.

"Oh, is that so, is that all?" Ronan replied, sarcastically.

"We have more planned of course, much more than you can ever imagine."

Hearing Dylan's words made Ronan almost freeze in fear. *Who knew all the atrocities that he had planned?*

"My followers and I are going to have so much fun especially with what we've already done."

"What do you mean?" he asked, his face paling.

"Didn't you notice that the city's blood supply has been disappearing lately and mortals have been showing up dead?"

"That was you?" Ronan asked, in shock.

"Who else did you think was responsible for all that?"

"You monster! my wife is dead because of you."

"Collateral damage."

Ronan climbed off of Dylan, he then grabbed him by the collar and threw him against one of the outer walls of the building. Walking over, he picked him up effortlessly and began to deliver a series of blows. He continued until Dylan having held back most of his strength up until that moment, extended his very sharp claws and his face became more lupine in appearance. He swiped at Ronan's face, momentarily blinding him, which gave him the chance he needed. He flipped them over once again and he swiped twice more across Ronan's chest severely injuring him. He then climbed off of Ronan and got away.

A few minutes later, once he felt that everything had healed, Ronan slowly sat up, *how did he fail to even consider that Dylan was ever anything besides mortal? There was no way, thinking back. Certain things should have set off alarms in his head, he should have known better.* Once he felt that he was ready to head back, he climbed to his feet and back towards the others.

1

# CHAPTER ELEVEN

Walking back towards the doors, Ronan was met once again with his remaining family and friends. Noticing that he was covered in blood, and that he had two deep

gashes across his chest, Mackenzie ran up to him and wrapped their arms around his frame. Slowly, Ronan raised a hand and cupped the back of his head, pulling them towards him. They stood like that for a while until Miles walked up and spoke up.

"Ronan is he dead?" he asked.

Gazing up into his eyes, Ronan shook his head.

"He managed to get away."

"How did you let him get away?" Miles asked.

He looked at Miles in disbelief.

"Get away? I didn't let him get away!" Ronan exclaimed.

"Oh really, how so?"

Breaking away from where he stood with Mackenzie, Ronan walked over to Miles until the two of them stood nose to nose.

"He momentarily blinded me with his claws."

"Claws? What do you mean Ronan?" Xavier asked, stepping out from where he stood behind Miles.

"I don't know how but it is. He's both a Lycan and a Nightwalker somehow."

"So, he's a hybrid then?"

Ronan nodded.

"Most likely."

"I'm sorry, Ronan. I jumped to conclusions, I don't understand how he can be both a Lycan and Nightwalker."

"Well he said his father was Jackson, his mother must have been a Nightwalker," Xavier said.

"Where's Chase is he alright?" he asked, looking around.

1

Mackenzie nodded.

"C'mon, I'll bring you to him," they said, gesturing for Ronan to follow them.

◆◆◆

They made their way through the crowd until they found Chase laying with his head on Mackenzie's backpack. Walking over, the two of them knelt by him. Ronan gave him a once over, checking to see if he had any physical wounds.

"How are you feeling?" he asked Chase.

Grimacing, Chase shrugged.

"Kind of sore, to be honest. Is it true, is Cole actually dead?" he asked.

Ronan nodded.

"I'm glad the bite took," Ronan replied, he reached out and pulled the collar of Chase's shirt aside, taking a look at Chase's bite.

"Am I going to be okay?"

"Of course, don't worry. I'm your sire, it's my duty to look after you and make sure you can manage as a Daywalker."

"Really?"

"Of course."

"Thank you, Ronan."

Ronan wrapped his arms around Chase's body and pulled him into a hug.

Over the course of the following month, everyone began to help rebuild what was lost. Chase was recovering rather nicely and thankfully slowly adjusting as a Daywalker, as everyone helped where and how they could.

1

# EPILOGUE

I had been a month since their last encounter with Dylan and there were murmurs that the Sanguists were regrouping their numbers spreading to various parts of the country. I needed to talk to some allies to see if they could help us. At the moment, I was in my study on the phone when finally a few minutes later, I heard a voice on the other end of the phone.

"Hello?" a man's voice travelled through the phone.

"Am I speaking to Matteo?" I asked.

"Yes, who's this?"

The voice on the other end seemed to be curious as to who would be calling and especially at this hour.

"It's Ronan. I'm not sure if you remember me?"

"Of course, I do. How are your kids? I think I remember Theo mentioning them."

Taking a moment, Ronan felt his throat close up. Swallowing hard, he continued with great difficulty.

1

"That's why I called. Something happened, and we really need your help, Matteo."

"Say no more. I'll talk to everyone here and we'll fly out by the end of the week."

"You will?"

"Yea, I'll keep you updated during the week, Ronan. We'll talk later, okay?"

"But don't you want to know what happened?" I ask.

"You wouldn't call unless it was important. Don't worry you can tell me what happened when you get here," Matteo replied.

"Okay will do. Bye Matteo."

"Have a safe flight and take care. I'll see you when you guys get here." "I hung up the phone and began to make all the necessary preparations we needed before we headed to Vancouver. I honestly didn't know how we were going to defeat Dylan only that we needed to take care of getting rid of him and his followers and restoring peace and freedom back to the country that they had overtaken.

Reaching over my desk, I picked up the bottle that sat upon the top of it and poured myself a generous amount of whisky that was in it. Raising the glass to my lips, I took a long drink and then placed the glass down, sighing deeply, knowing that I had a huge problem ahead of me now.

1

Nancy A. Lopes

# AboutTheAuthor

Nancy A. Lopes is the award-winning, bestselling author of The Immortal Chronicles series. She graduated from George Brown College in April 2016 with a certificate in Novel Writing. You can follow her on Twitter at @nancyalopes, on Instagram at @nancyalopes, and her Facebook page https://www.facebook.com/nancyalopes/ She is always eager to hear from any fans.

www.ingramcontent.com/pod-product-compliance
Lightning Source LLC
Chambersburg PA
CBHW060425260626
47161CB00005B/1790